CLANCY
THE LONESOME LITTLE DONKEY

JOHN R. TWEEDY

Archway Publishing books may be ordered through booksellers or by contacting:

Archway Publishing
1663 Liberty Drive
Bloomington, IN 47403
www.archwaypublishing.com
1 (888) 242-5904

ISBN: 978-1-4808-4075-1 (sc)
ISBN: 978-1-4808-4077-5 (e)
ISBN: 978-1-4808-4076-8 (hc)

Print information available on the last page.

Archway Publishing rev. date: 1/13/2017

Once upon a time, there was a little
donkey whose name was Clancy.

Clancy lived on a very poor farm. He had little to eat other than a few weeds, and he drank out of an old wooden bucket. Most of his days, he sat idly beneath a worn and tired apple tree and watched the beautiful racehorses in the flowered fields right next door.

How he longed to be a racehorse! But of course, he knew he did not look like a racehorse. His coat was muddy. His tail and mane were covered in burrs. Everything about him was old and dirty. Even the old shed he slept in was so crooked that it might fall down at any moment, and also, the roof leaked badly whenever it rained. Then he became wet! Life was very difficult; however, mostly he was just lonesome.

Mr. Scruggs, the mean old man who owned Clancy, used to make him work very hard pulling a big, heavy wagon loaded with rags and papers. Sometimes Scruggs would even whip him to make him go faster! Oh well! Mr. Scruggs no longer made him do anything anymore. The little man just sat on his front porch and whittled on pieces of wood. So Clancy just sat under the old apple tree and dreamed of becoming a racehorse.

Once in a while, to Clancy's delight, a great black racehorse named Big Jiggs would walk near Clancy's wire fence; however, the fence was always between them! Mostly Big Jiggs just stood in the shade of a fine, big maple tree and switched his tail at the flies that buzzed about him. Even his beautiful field of clover and lovely flowers caused him little interest. Big Jiggs was lonely too. All the races he had won didn't mean much when he didn't have anyone to share it with. Oh, if only he had a friend!

One day, as Clancy sat dreaming of the fine life he wished he might live, a man walked into Mr. Scruggs's front yard and asked if he might buy the one little donkey seated out under the apple tree.

Clancy's big, long ears stood almost straight up! He could not believe what he was hearing! *Who would want to buy me?* Still, Clancy heard Scruggs's strong voice say, "Sure, I'll sell him. He's no use to me!"

Thus it was that Clancy had a new owner. His name was Mr. Hanson, and what a kind and gentle man he was! Together they walked away, leaving the poor Old Scruggs's farm behind. Clancy had never felt happier!

Oh, what fine smells in the air as they neared Mr. Hanson's stables! The little shaded path that led to the Hanson Farm soon became fragrant with scents of flowers, clover, fresh-mown hay, saddle soap, and liniments. There were many new and different animal smells filling the air too. It all smelled so good!

Arriving at Mr. Hanson's big barn, Clancy became aware of ever so many animals scurrying about. There were dogs and cats, of course!

But there were also chickens, rabbits, goats, sheep, a monkey, and even a parrot that talked. Clancy soon learned that each of these new friends were also a friend to one of the many other racing horses.

Clancy was head over heels happy. No
one was ever lonesome here!

Mr. Hanson turned Clancy over to one of the stable boys of this big farm. The boy's name was William, but everyone called him Willy. "Here's a new friend for you, Willy," said Mr. Hanson. "After a cleaning, turn him into the pasture with Big Jiggs. I think they will become good friends." Then the kindly Mr. Hanson was gone.

First Willy washed and cleaned those big ears of Clancy's. Then Willy brushed and brushed and brushed Clancy's coat, and then he combed Clancy's mane and tail to get rid of all the many burrs that had been there for such a long, long, long time!

Then Willy gave Clancy a big bucket of fresh, clean water. After all those mud puddles, it tasted so *delicious!*

Now," said Willy, "I'll open the gate, and you scoot and make a friend of Big Jiggs."

As the gate opened, the big black horse ran to them. Big Jiggs slid to a stop and slowly sniffed at Clancy's nose. Suddenly, Big Jiggs remembered his little friend from across the fence.

Together they whirled and raced into the meadow of clover and flowers. They ran and kicked up their heels and even jumped high into the air until they were both so tired they went into Big Jiggs's stall and rolled in the clean, fresh bedding of straw. How happy they both were!

The big black horse was so happy that he even enjoyed racing again, and Clancy went with him and thought it so much fun to watch Big Jiggs win time after time.

After every race that Big Jiggs won, Clancy would shout, "Hee-haw, hee-haw!" The people would all laugh and laugh at the funny little fellow. Then Clancy would kick up his own stubby little tail. Never had Clancy enjoyed such a good time!

Willy once even hung the roses that Big Jiggs had won upon Clancy's neck. He felt so very important—and he was! But Clancy wasn't really aware of his own importance.

THE END

One day, if you are out for a drive in the country and you see a big black horse and a wee donkey sitting side by side under a fine maple tree, just say, "Hee-haw, hee-haw!" And if the little donkey answers you, it might just be Clancy—now a happy little donkey!

Dedication

This book is dedicated to all little children and children at heart, including my granddaughter, Rebecca! This book would never have seen the light of day without her. The sketches in this book were done over twenty years ago. They sat in a manila envelope for decades until Rebecca found them and brought them to life. While spending some time sketching at the race track, I was completely enamored with the special relationship between race horses and their companion animals. I was able to see first-hand dogs, goats, sheep, chickens, piglets and even talking parrots living side by side with the horses. These "companion animals" had a very special purpose - to be the race horse's BFF, or "best friend forever", so the horses would be happier and less anxious.

About the Author

*Author John R. Tweedy pictured
with granddaughter Rebecca*

John R. Tweedy was born and raised in upstate New York where he spent his formative years fishing, drawing, and painting. Throughout his life, he has delighted children, grandchildren, and friends with whimsical sketches, often drawn on placemats or random slips of paper. *Clancy the Lonesome Little Donkey* is his first book.

CPSIA information can be obtained
at www.ICGtesting.com
Printed in the USA
LVOW05s1620290617

539640LV00027B/717/P

9 781480 840751